# THE NIGHT BEFORE CHRISTMAS

## A POEM BY CLEMENT C. MOORE

## WILL MOSES

PHILOMEL BOOKS

## Dear Reader,

When I was living at home, just about every Christmas Eve my cousin Harry would stop in for a visit and we would all enjoy hearing Harry, a natural storyteller, recite his collection of stories and events. We would sit in front of the great fieldstone fireplace that my father enjoyed so much and we would watch the lights twinkle on the ragged and oversized white pine tree that I had chopped down earlier and now seemed to engulf the room.

   Maybe we would enjoy some popcorn and hot chocolate as the evening ticked by. For me, though, Christmas Eve was a night of high anticipation, a night when each passing hour seemed like a week. For all the while, starting at about seven in the morning on the twenty-fourth of December, it would be heavy on my mind that the very next morning was Christmas Day. Christmas morning was my goal; it was then that I could finally find out what was in all those colorful packages under the tree and, even better, discover what Santa Claus put in my stocking!

But on Christmas Eve, all that seemed ever so far away to me. Then, just as I could hardly stand the anticipation any longer, my mother would get out the old and tattered *The Night Before Christmas* book, the one illustrated by my great-grandmother, Grandma Moses, and read the famous poem by Clement C. Moore, a reading that wasn't always appreciated by me at the time, as I somehow viewed this as one more roadblock to Christmas morning and presents.

As I look back now, though, I really don't remember much about what was in any of those packages, but it seems I do remember the simple warm rituals and traditions that were being fashioned in me at the time. Many years have gone by, and my wife, Sharon, and I have kids of our own. Every Christmas Eve, Sharon gets out the same old *The Night Before Christmas* and reads it to our kids. And every Christmas Eve, we have a fire in the fireplace and I am happy to say that Cousin Harry still comes up for a visit, stories, some supper and popcorn.

I had some reservations about illustrating *The Night Before Christmas* because in my mind it was a Grandma Moses story, and even today people tell me how much that book meant to them when they were little. Oftentimes, though, they would say the book is all worn-out and ask, "When are you going to illustrate the poem?" Well, as you can see, I finally got around to the task. All I can hope for is that the generation that grows up on my version takes it with them through their lives as a good memory from an earlier Christmas and, just as with me, it becomes part of the fabric of which their family traditions are woven.

Merry Christmas!

*Will Moses*

*To Old St. Nick: You've been good to a lot of us!*

’Twas the night before Christmas, when all through the house

Not a creature was stirring,
not even a mouse.

The stockings were hung
by the chimney with care,

In hopes that St. Nicholas
soon would be there;

The children were nestled
all snug in their beds,

While visions of sugar-plums
danced in their heads;

And mamma in her 'kerchief,
and I in my cap,

Had just settled our brains
for a long winter's nap,

When out on the lawn
there arose such a clatter,

I sprang from the bed
to see what was the matter.

14

Away to the window
I flew like a flash,

Tore open the shutters
and threw up the sash.

The moon on the breast
of the new-fallen snow

Gave the lustre of mid-day
to objects below,

When, what to my wondering eyes should appear,

But a miniature sleigh, and eight tiny reindeer,

With a little old driver, so lively and quick,

I knew in a moment it must be St. Nick.

More rapid than eagles his coursers they came,

And he whistled, and shouted, and called them by name;

"Now, Dasher! Now, Dancer! Now, Prancer and Vixen!

On, Comet! On, Cupid! On, Donder and Blitzen!

19

To the top of the porch! To the top of the wall!

Now dash away! Dash away! Dash away all!"

As dry leaves that before
    the wild hurricane fly,

When they meet with an obstacle,
    mount to the sky,

So up to the house-top
    the coursers they flew,

With the sleigh full of toys,
    and St. Nicholas too.

And then, in a twinkling,
    I heard on the roof

The prancing and pawing
    of each little hoof.

As I drew in my head,
    and was turning around,

Down the chimney St. Nicholas came with a bound.

He was dressed all in fur, from his head to his foot,

And his clothes were all tarnished with ashes and soot;

A bundle of toys he had flung on his back,

And he looked like a peddler just opening his pack.

His eyes—how they twinkled!
　　His dimples how merry!

His cheeks were like roses,
　　his nose like a cherry!

His droll little mouth
　　was drawn up like a bow,

And the beard of his chin
　　was as white as the snow;

The stump of a pipe
　　he held tight in his teeth,

And the smoke it encircled
　　his head like a wreath;

He had a broad face and a little round belly,

That shook, when he laughed, like a bowlful of jelly.

He was chubby and plump, a right jolly old elf,

And I laughed when I saw him, in spite of myself;

A wink of his eye and a twist of his head,

Soon gave me to know I had nothing to dread;

He spoke not a word, but went straight to his work,

And filled all the stockings; then turned with a jerk,

And laying his finger aside of his nose,

And giving a nod, up the chimney he rose;

He sprang to his sleigh, to his team gave a whistle,

And away they all flew like the down of a thistle.

But I heard him exclaim, ere he drove out of sight,

"HAPPY CHRISTMAS TO ALL,
AND TO ALL A GOOD-NIGHT!"

Patricia Lee Gauch, editor

**PHILOMEL BOOKS**
A division of Penguin Young Readers Group.
Published by The Penguin Group.
Penguin Group (USA) Inc., 375 Hudson Street, New York, NY 10014, U.S.A.
Penguin Group (Canada), 90 Eglinton Avenue East, Suite 700, Toronto, Ontario, Canada M4P 2Y3
(a division of Pearson Penguin Canada Inc.).
Penguin Books Ltd, 80 Strand, London WC2R 0RL, England.
Penguin Ireland, 25 St. Stephen's Green, Dublin 2, Ireland (a division of Penguin Books Ltd.).
Penguin Group (Australia), 250 Camberwell Road, Camberwell, Victoria 3124, Australia (a division of Pearson Australia Group Pty Ltd).
Penguin Books India Pvt Ltd, 11 Community Centre, Panchsheel Park, New Delhi - 110 017, India.
Penguin Group (NZ), Cnr Airborne and Rosedale Roads, Albany, Auckland 1310, New Zealand (a division of Pearson New Zealand Ltd).
Penguin Books (South Africa) (Pty) Ltd, 24 Sturdee Avenue, Rosebank, Johannesburg 2196, South Africa.
Penguin Books Ltd, Registered Offices: 80 Strand, London WC2R 0RL, England.

Design by Semadar Megged.   Text set in 20-point Goudy.   The art was done in oil on Fabriano paper.

Library of Congress Cataloging-in-Publication Data
Moore, Clement Clarke, 1779–1863.
The night before Christmas / Clement C. Moore ; illustrated by Will Moses. p. cm.
1. Santa Claus—Juvenile poetry. 2. Christmas—Juvenile poetry. 3. Children's poetry, American. I. Moses, Will, ill. II. Title.
PS2429.M5N5 2006c    811'.2—dc22    2005032646

ISBN 0-399-23745-3
1 3 5 7 9 10 8 6 4 2
First Impression